KT-497-625

Celebrate Kipper's 18th birthday with other Kipper books:

Kipper
Kipper's Toybox
Kipper's Birthday
Kipper's Monster
Kipper and Roly
Kipper's Beach Ball

Storyboards:

Butterfly	Castle
Hisssss!	Miaow!
Honk!	Playtime!
Splosh!	Swing!

THIS BOOK BELONGS TO:

Picnic

Mick Inkpen

A division of Hachette Children's Books

Everything was ready for the picnic on top of Big Hill.

'Let's eat!' said Kipper. 'Jam or cheese?'

But before he could take a bite. . .

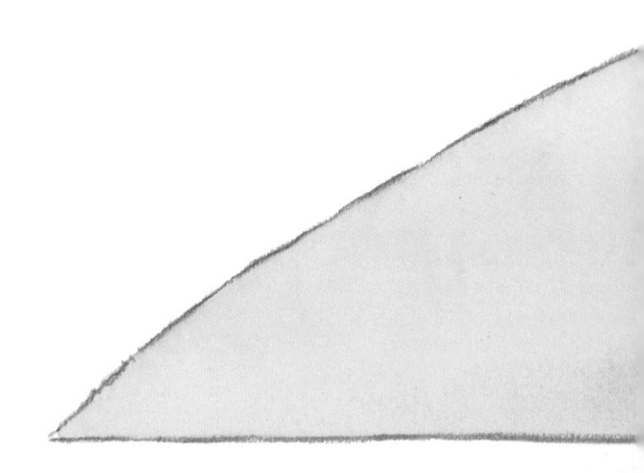

‘Wheee! Look at it go!’ It was Pig, playing with Arnold’s kite.

‘Watch out, Pig!’

But Pig was too busy to notice. He tramped right through the picnic. So did Arnold.

‘Let’s go to the pond,’ said Tiger.

They set out the picnic again.

'Cheese or jam?' said Kipper. But Tiger didn't reply. Instead he screamed, and jumped into the pond!

'Ants!' he said, pointing at Kipper.

It wasn't just the ants that wanted the picnic. The ducks were hungry too.

'Shoo!' said Kipper. 'Go away!'

Tiger gave his soggy sandwich to the duck.

'Let's try somewhere else,' he said.

Now there were only two sandwiches left.

'Jam or cheese?' said Kipper.

'Ooh, jam!' said Tiger. 'I love jam!'

Unfortunately, so did the wasps.

They ran into Pig. He looked upset.

'The kite!' he said. 'It's stuck in a tree!' He cheered up though, when he saw the sandwich. The last sandwich.

'Oooh! Is that going spare?' he said, and stuffed it into his mouth, all in one go!

Kipper was cross, but not quite as cross as Tiger.

When they had calmed down, Pig led them to the place where Arnold's kite was stuck.

They all shook the tree. . .

Down came Arnold's kite.
And down came lots
and lots
of big,
red,
shiny
apples.

There were more apples
than they could eat.

First published in 2001 by Hodder Children's Books
A division of Hachette Children's Books, 338 Euston Road, London, NW1 3BH

Hachette Children's Books Australia, Level 17/207 Kent Street, Sydney, NSW 2000

Illustrations by Stuart Trotter

A catalogue record of this book is available from the British Library.

ISBN: 978 0 340 78850 9
10 9 8 7 6 5 4 3 2

Printed in China

Hodder Children's Books is a division of Hachette Children's Books
An Hachette Livre UK Company